Squirrel Nutkin

Retold by
Sarah Toast

Cover illustrated by
Anita Nelson

Book illustrated by
Pat Schoonover

Based on the original story by Beatrix Potter with all new illustrations.

Copyright © 1995 Publications International, Ltd.
All rights reserved. This book may not be reproduced or quoted in whole or in part by mimeograph or any other printed or electronic means, or for presentation on radio, television, videotape, or film without written permission from

Louis Weber, C.E.O.
Publications International, Ltd.
7373 North Cicero Avenue
Lincolnwood, Illinois 60646

Permission is never granted for commercial purposes.

Manufactured in U.S.A.

8 7 6 5 4 3 2 1

ISBN: 0-7853-2205-1

PUBLICATIONS INTERNATIONAL, LTD.
Rainbow is a trademark of Publications International, Ltd.

This is a tale about a tail—a tail that belonged to a little red squirrel named Nutkin. He had a brother called Twinkleberry and a great many cousins. Nutkin, Twinkleberry, and all their cousins lived in the woods at the edge of a lake.

In the middle of the lake, there was an island covered with trees and nut bushes. Among the trees stood a hollow oak tree. An owl called Old Brown lived in that hollow tree and looked over the island.

One fall day, when the leaves on the hazelnut bushes were gold and green and the nuts were ripe, Nutkin and Twinkleberry and all the other little squirrels came out of the woods. The squirrels gathered down at the edge of the lake.

They made little rafts out of twigs. Then they paddled over the water to Owl Island, hoping to gather nuts. Each squirrel had a little sack and a big oar. All the squirrels spread out their tails for sails.

The squirrels also took with them a present of three mice for Old Brown. Twinkleberry said politely to Mr. Brown, "Will you kindly allow us to gather nuts?" But Nutkin pranced around singing a squeaky song.

Mr. Brown just went to sleep. Then the squirrels all filled their little sacks with nuts and sailed back home.

The next morning they returned. Twinkleberry brought Old Brown a fat mole. He asked, "Mr. Brown, will you kindly let us gather more nuts?"

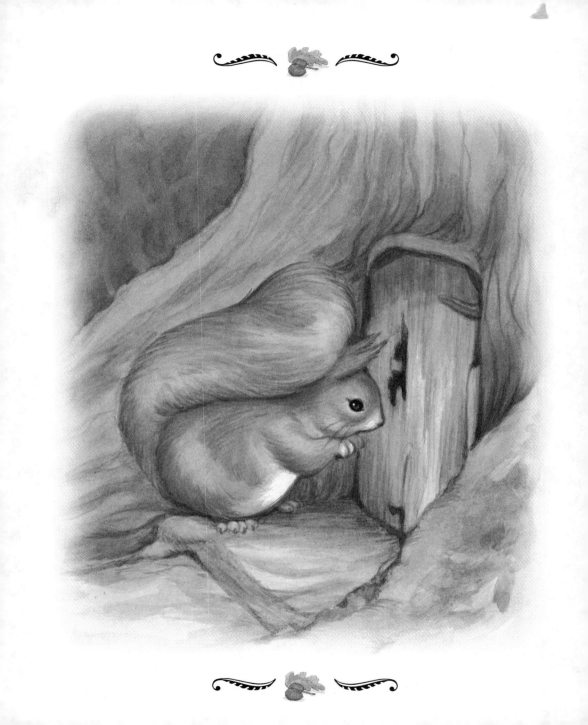

But Nutkin did not behave. He danced up and down, tickling Old Brown with a leaf. Then Nutkin sang a very silly song.

Mr. Brown woke up suddenly and carried the mole into his house. When he shut the door, Nutkin began singing a song through the keyhole!

While the other squirrels searched the island for nuts to put in their little sacks, Nutkin gathered small pebbles and played on a stump where he could watch Old Brown's door.

On the third day the squirrels woke up very early and went fishing. They soon caught seven fat minnows. Then they paddled across the lake and landed under a tree on Owl Island.

Twinkleberry and six other little squirrels each brought a fat minnow to Old Brown. But Nutkin brought no present. He ran in front of the others singing a silly song.

The squirrels filled their sacks with nuts, but Nutkin played a game of rolling pebbles at pinecones.

On the next day the squirrels brought honey to Mr. Brown. Nutkin skipped up and down, singing a really silly song.

On the fifth day the squirrels went to Owl Island for the last time. As a present for Old Mr. Brown, they brought a fresh egg in a little round basket. But Nutkin bobbed up and down laughing and shouting.

Mr. Brown liked eggs enough to open one eye. Then he shut it quickly without saying anything.

Nutkin danced up and down like a sunbeam, but Old Brown still kept silent.

Then Nutkin began to chant as rudely as ever,

> The man in the wilderness
>   said to me,
> "How many strawberries
>   grow in the sea?"
> I answered him as
>   I thought good—
> "As many red herrings
>   as grow in the wood."

The squirrels watched Nutkin, not knowing how Old Brown would react.

As if that were not enough naughtiness for one day, Nutkin made a whirring noise and danced in circles. Then he took a running jump right onto Old Brown's head!

Mr. Brown had finally had enough. All at once there was a fluttering and a scuffling and a loud squeak! The other squirrels quickly bolted into the bushes to hide.

When the squirrels crept back, they peeked around the oak tree. There was Old Brown sitting on his doorstep.

Old Mr. Brown sat quite still with his eyes closed, as if nothing had happened. But Nutkin was tucked under his wing!

Mr. Brown carried Nutkin into his house. He held Nutkin by the tail as he set a pot of water on to boil.

Nutkin did not want to stay for supper. He pulled from Old Brown's grip so hard that his tail broke in two. As fast as he could, Nutkin dashed up the stairs and jumped out a window of Mr. Brown's tree.

To this day, if you see Nutkin up in a tree, and you sing him a song and ask him a riddle, he will throw sticks and stamp his feet and scold, "Cuck-cuck-cuck-cur-r-r-cuck-k-k!"